BEAVER'S
~BIG~
ADVENTURE

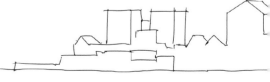

Magnus Weightman

BEAVER'S ~BIG~ ADVENTURE

 FIVE QUILLS

Beaver lived near a dam in a house built of wood,
And dreamt of adventures whenever he could.

Then one sunny day, he set off to explore.
"Goodbye, everyone! Goodbye, river shore!"

Beaver floated past forests, he slept under the sky.
He rushed along rapids, he admired views from up high.

He paddled a long way, all on his own . . .

. . . when suddenly he thought, "How do I find my way home?"

Just then a hot-air balloon offered him a ride.

Akita the dog said, "I'll be your guide!"

"Wow!" Beaver cried, as they floated up high.

"The Earth looks incredible from up here in the sky!"

Akita was curious – he'd never met a beaver before.
Where was his home? Was it down there on the shore?

"Beaver, is that your house hidden in the snow down there?"
"No, Akita, that's the home of the seal and the polar bear."

"Is your house dug deep under an oak tree?"
"No, that is where the foxes live, wild and free."

"Beaver, do you make sweet honey in your home?"
"No, Queen Bee and her swarm made this magnificent comb."

"Look, a ball woven from straw. Could that be your house?"

"No, that is the work of a minute harvest mouse."

"Come, Beaver, let's enjoy the view from the stork's cosy nest.
Let's take some time to rest before we continue our quest."

"Do you live in a tower made of earth, twigs and sand?"

"No, it's the tiny termites that made something so grand."

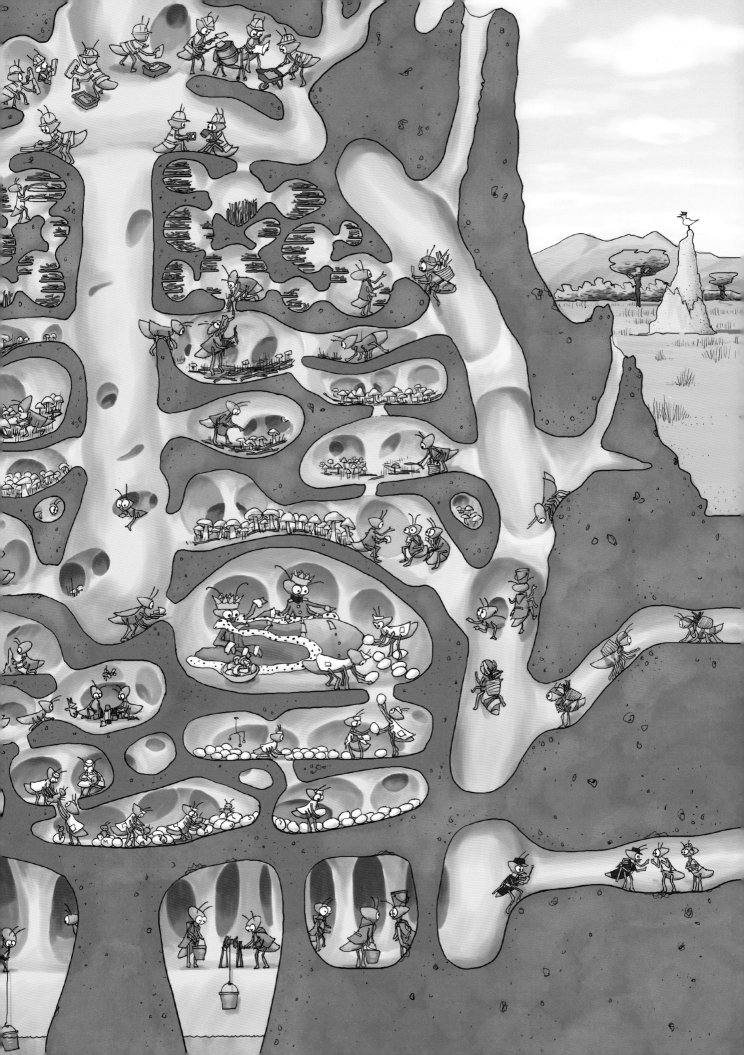

"Is your house made from grass? Does it hang from a tree?"
"No, the weaverbird made this for his family, you see."

"Do you live in this romantic and colourful love nest?"

"The bowerbird built this, Akita, and his sweetheart is impressed."

"Do you live in a shell house with your friends by the sea?"
"No, hermit crabs carry their home on their back, not me."

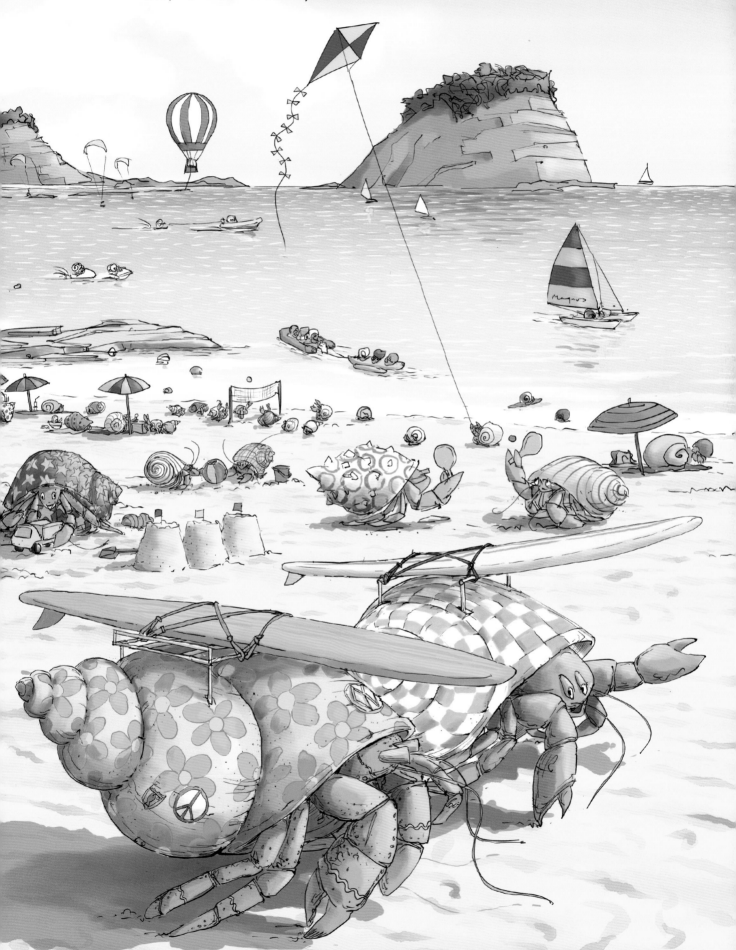

"Do you live in a rock cave on the seabed?"
"No, the tilefish and their friends live here instead."

"Beaver, do you live in a town underground?"

"Not me, Akita – this is where the prairie dogs are found."

"Do you live near a dam, Beaver, in a house built of wood?"

"Yes! Yes, I do!" Beaver couldn't stop grinning – seeing home felt so good.

"Thank you, Akita, you are a true friend.
You showed me the world, you brought me home in the end."

At home at last – everyone is there.
Beaver is excited, he has many wonderful stories to share!

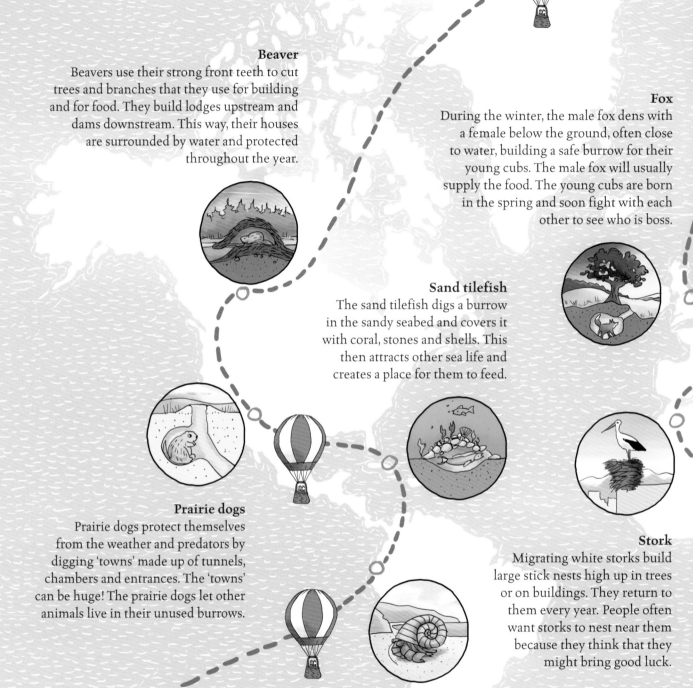

Beaver

Beavers use their strong front teeth to cut trees and branches that they use for building and for food. They build lodges upstream and dams downstream. This way, their houses are surrounded by water and protected throughout the year.

Fox

During the winter, the male fox dens with a female below the ground, often close to water, building a safe burrow for their young cubs. The male fox will usually supply the food. The young cubs are born in the spring and soon fight with each other to see who is boss.

Sand tilefish

The sand tilefish digs a burrow in the sandy seabed and covers it with coral, stones and shells. This then attracts other sea life and creates a place for them to feed.

Prairie dogs

Prairie dogs protect themselves from the weather and predators by digging 'towns' made up of tunnels, chambers and entrances. The 'towns' can be huge! The prairie dogs let other animals live in their unused burrows.

Stork

Migrating white storks build large stick nests high up in trees or on buildings. They return to them every year. People often want storks to nest near them because they think that they might bring good luck.

Hermit crabs

Hermit crabs protect their soft bodies with empty seashells, left behind mostly by sea snails. When the crab grows in size, it must find a larger shell and leave the previous one. Sometimes the crabs swap shells with each other.

Polar bear and seal

Mother polar bears hibernate with their cubs during the winter months, until spring arrives. Male polar bears, however, roam about if there is plenty of food available. Seals build snow dens on pack ice off the coast to breed their pups.

Honeybee

Honeybees suck up nectar from flowers, turning it into honey. Then they eat the honey to make beeswax. Worker bees place the beeswax on the branches of a tree and shape it into a honeycomb.

Harvest mouse

Harvest mice carefully weave grass and attached stems into round breeding nests well above the ground to protect themselves and their young from their many predators.

Bowerbird

Male bowerbirds build bowers and arrange a beautiful collection of fruits, flowers or found objects, particularly with bright colours, to attract a female. But these are not used as nests for living in.

Termites

Termites are only a few millimetres long, but they can build mounds ten metres high. The mounds have an amazing ventilation system to keep their food storage, fungi gardens and nurseries not too cold, not too warm, but at just the right temperature.

Weaverbird

To avoid monkeys stealing eggs or their young, male weaverbirds weave a round nest with leaves on a branch. If the female likes the nest, she helps to complete the entrance and interior.

For Bjarne, Finn and Matilda

Special thanks to Silke, Chris, Christina,
Edwin, Majka, Evi, Bernd, and Mum and Dad

And to Esther van der Werf for the Dutch text
for Welkom thuis, Bever!

BEAVER'S BIG ADVENTURE

Welkom Thuis, Bever!
First published in Belgium and the Netherlands in 2017 by
Clavis Uitgeverij, Hasselt-Amsterdam-New York.

This edition published in Great Britain in 2019 by Five Quills
93 Oakwood Court, London W14 8JZ
www.fivequills.co.uk
Five Quills and associated logos are trademarks of Five Quills Ltd.

Text and illustrations copyright © 2017 Clavis Uitgeverij,
Hasselt-Amsterdam-New York. All rights reserved.
UK English edition text edited by Natascha Biebow at Blue Elephant Storyshaping

A CIP record for this title is available from the British Library

ISBN 978-0-9935537-7-6

1 3 5 7 9 10 8 6 4 2

Printed in Croatia by INK69

FIVE
QUILLS